Feelings from my Heart and Soul II

Feelings from my *Heart* and *Soul* II

A WONDERFUL JOURNEY OF A POET

June 20, 2019

Dear Tom,
You are a wonderful friend and I shall love you to the very end.
Happy Birthday and many more. 75th I do Adore!
Enjoy my book. Hope you get hooked! :
Celebrate Life!

Love,
Andy

ANDREA LAMBERTSON

urlink
PRINT & MEDIA

1603 Capitol Ave., Suite 310 Cheyenne, Wyoming USA 82001
1-888-980-6523 | admin@urlinkpublishing.com

URLink Print and Media is committed to excellence in the publishing industry.

Published in the United States of America

ISBN 978-1-64367-516-9 (Paperback)
ISBN 978-1-64367-515-2 (Digital)

17.05.19

To all who love nature and
our environment

Contents

Petals Of Dignity

I hold a piece of nature in the palm of my hand
And feel centered by this creation.
Life is not always a prickly stem.
These soft petals speak dignity and truth
Behind which we should not hide,
Only should a storm arise.
Embrace its fragrance, purity and protection.

In the center of life are delicacies
Like pistil and stamen centered in this flower.
We protect them, sometimes to our advantage,
Sometimes to our detriment.

Blossoms grow in groups for strength and courage.
They bask in sunlight, they grow thick and rich.
They may lose a petal or two,
But with fresh soil and nutriments, revive.
You too may lose a petal, perhaps a few,
But with insight and the help of friends,
Like fragile flower petals, will renew.

'Tis I

I am so thankful dear Lord
When thoughts do flow from my mind and my heart
You enhance my heart, you enhance my glow
The light within me comes out in this form
Of phonics and rhyme
With this gift I was born
Please direct this gift toward security and such
Make sure I know I am really in touch
With the body and blood of our dear Jesus Christ
I kneel and pray for guidance, yes advice

Where do we go from here my friend?
How would you like me with society/community to blend?

I listen, I wait
Smother the temperament, abate debate
Please dear Lord help me open the gate
To the environment and people of which I am now a part
I am ready, willing, and able with the Father, Son, Holy
        Spirit, and Blessed Mary
To start!

Warmth

The warmth of a fire
The warmth of the sun

The warmth of a lover The warmth of a friend

All should embrace and never should cease
For us may we always have love, happiness and peace.

Searching

Oh the lonely night so quiet and still
Nary a breeze, nary a chill
The crickets play their song on high
I wish to see a heaven rest before my eyes
My thoughts my mind are the only friends I have
Each alone and together, mystifyingly sad.

A breeze, a breathe of hope
Should they never come near
Upon her knees she prays for a love so dear
There has always been a beginning, a middle, and an end
At which point am I in life
Shall I start again?

The wound is deep, it may never heal
Searching, searching, searching for thoughts that appeal
The journey is a long one I've been told Time—Life—
Happiness hope to enfold!

Someday

Sand sea surf serene sky— someday die
Mist mirth mounds mental— maybe someday soon
Sight sound silence sooth
Effortless ebony— do not move
Memories mighty more of these
Questions, answers how I plead!

Winter Feeling

Not a day goes by when I look at the sky
Blue yet not blue as we may seem
This color indeed incites many a dream

Those beautiful white flakes, for goodness sake
Stir and whirl like that beautiful dancing girl
It may be on the ice or slopes of the mountain top
But we always must think cream of the crop
I drop, stop and think.

Of successful ways to combine, you know
The kind, sublime, unwind kind of time
We all love the cold for we know warmth
will eventually unfold
I've been told not to be so bold.

This would be unheard of, untold
So please sit back and watch the birds fly up in the sky
I can not tell a lie
I love winter time!

Where Do We Go From Here

Where do we go from here
Mid life's crisis all of a sudden appears
Values accrue
No more to say I do
Rather, I am and understand
The vicissitudes of life
Common to all, our givens
Of happy moments and those of strife.

Feelings I never knew I had
To create peace and happiness
As a returned smile makes you glad

The simple requests when taken to task
I feel at least, I asked
Not all comes through for you or for me
I am happy to be one of nature's appreciators
The fresh air that I breathe
A lost soul to retrieve.

A thoughtful moment in prayer
Do I dare say I love life
Its goodness and its strife.
Yes, Life and Love
Helps us all, at any age, at any stage
And so as time passes, may we see the light.

A Winter's Snow

Oh, How I love a winter's snow
To walk amid the white statues
Sculptures made by a special heir
      The bushes like cactus
      with sharp prickly spines
The trees are naked their branches entwined
      The feeling of being alone
      Oh ever so divine
      The ice, yes it is frozen
      With a blanket of white
      Oh— how in love I am with this night.
Sounds still travel over hill and vale
The land has changed its complexion
      To a very shade of pale.
It is not a an unhappy complexion you see
It is very content to be alone with me.
      Whenever one so ever wants
      Peace with the world
      Walk a path of white
      Which covers the ground
You will see there are very few human beings
      to be found
      Yes, if one you find has
      Venture forth in the
      same search as you have.

Freeze your hearts together
    Rest your bodies near for warmth
    Let your lips melt and your eyes see together
Two minds have loved a winter snow.

Late In The Winter
Begins Soon The Spring

The trees bearing coin silver on the magnificence of their
      bark
They are outstanding silhouettes as the moon light touches
their skin

Direct neighbor is a graceful pine swaying in the wind to
      the
side of the dock
Pale shades of brown and silver and green
At this time of the year, reign supreme

Softness found in such a sight
My eyes are delighted as I absorb this night

A black crow rests on the hinges called branch
His eyes gliding across the creek
Does he dare find the chance to dine in the moonlight?

My heart feels wonderment as I gaze upward and see a star
filled sky
This evening, an emblem, not a disguise
A delightfully enjoyed surprise.

Forty Steps

The leaves have fallen on the ground
The ocean is quiet— not even a sound
The wind is at my back with a gentle push
The seagulls play a gleeful game
     in the marsh weeds and the bush.
The sound of the leaves
They rustle by with swift pace
My soul rises to the surface
mid life's race
The need for forty more steps to
     untie bad disgrace.
The misty horizon makes it clear
That adventure, the unknown will always appear.
The bay of tranquility rests before me,
     Not an ocean of storm
There are people so dear and
     so near and so warm.
Fresh is the air that I
breathe Clear is my
mind as I think
Let us all be so grateful for God's
plan for our lives
I am human being with spirit I am God's given man.
We who slide by showing
     never a cry

Do not succeed but become
     a weed—tangled
     torn, rooted and such—
I am not that way anymore.
I've changed—thanks Dear Lord
     so much.

A Journey

I followed the road through the tunnel of trees
In the Berkshires these on the right and left of me
The sunset was extraordinaire with colors so divine
Patterns of clouds you could not find
Such dynamics created by only one
Who in spirit we can relate and we can accelerate
Our beings all in one

It is not hard to concentrate if you really try
Have a burning desire to share with each and every one in
　　　the by and by
Reward yourself in heart and soul
Give everyone their happiness, content and relief in the
　　　form of a sigh
Structure, pattern, belief, peace, faith, confidence
All rest in the hearts of young and old

Problem— Victory Problem— Victory Problem— Victory
Hope Enfold!

A Cup Of Inspiration

My cup has a bird and flower motif which reminds me of my late fall journey to Mary Hammond O'Brien Houk's home. She lived in a wooded area and I was not too far away.

I loved visiting Mary once a week to help her with her home. She was eighty five years old—brilliant, well-read, a teacher, loved the art of fencing and a truly caring and giving woman. I looked forward to visiting her each time with my vacuum and duster. There was always a wonderful pay back and I do not mean money.

Upon completion of my work Mary would say, "Andréa, how about a cup of refrigerator soup?" Indeed, Mrs. Houk, I would love some! The delicious fragrant vapor from the soup pot permeated the room and I could not wait to be seated.

Into the speckled thick round cup with a curved handle, she would pour her divine concoction. On the cool fall days and cold winter afternoons the cup was most welcome. Potatoes, corn niblets, string beans, cauliflower, noodles, chicken bits and the "piece de resistance" was the taste of sherry.

Along with this cup of soup were the stories of Mary's life. Every detail included in each passage. She kindly asked how I was feeling and I replied with honesty. Indeed there was the taking in and giving out of magnificent thoughts, feelings, and experiences, but the give and take of the cup of refrigerator soup was awesome, wicked good!

Mary Houk just celebrated her 95th birthday in Bedford, Massachusetts. I attended the party given by her daughter, Sara Houk. A grand celebration

For a grand lady who indeed was famous for her gift of a cup of that good old American hospitality. Thank you Mary!

God bless you Mary and many more to come!

Christmas Eve 1998

I love you God with all my heart and soul
Many times and this you have been told
Yet I feel so comfortable saying each day
Without your help, I could no longer work or play

You shine through friends of mine
Your body and blood in the form of bread and wine
Sublime each time you extend yourself
You help those off the dusty shelf

Renewed again and not to worry
Renewed again and not to hurry
Baby steps
      Day by day
      Sunset to dawning

It is for your presence I pray
To guide— to lead
To help one take heed
In all you do and say

It is a sense of belonging
It is only this for which I am longing
Not to victimize, be critical but shhhhhhh

Peace / Contentment gifts of love for the world.

Let Us Walk Into The New Year 1999

Footsteps of red
Footsteps of gold
Footsteps with black and brown soles
Footsteps of patent, tasseled and white
Footsteps approach us each day and night

Footsteps of pink
Footsteps of blue
Which of the many footsteps are you?
Mine travel to the altar of God and share in the gifts to
     make him "Laud"

Footsteps big and those of which are small
Travel, indeed, the sacred halls
Footsteps gliding, sliding swift pace
For the body and blood of the human race

Give today for those who need what we can do for them
Walk more toward giving so that our lives and resources
     may be
Aimed at enemies as well as friends
At neighbors as well as strangers

Happy New Year!

An Easter Special

I have holly in my backyard and bunnies too
So this is a very special Easter Greeting for you
The stocking was hung by the chimney with care
For the Easter Spirit knew that a bunny would hop in there
He loves his holly it serves as a special treat
And reminds him of his friend Molly who lives down the
   street
Please do celebrate on this extremely blessed day
Special Easter Greetings are sent to you in many ways!

Summer Ends And Fall Begins

The summer winds came blowing in upon the shore
Our beach, pool, tennis courts, basketball cried for more
Kayaks and canoes, motor boats and fishing too
Such delight for guests and residents every day and every
     night

Time passed quickly, even on rainy days
Observe the farmer's cows and horses as they graze, I say
Good ole chaps we could be called
At present we are on our way to the fall

The leaves shall change
Birds, bees, frogs and all of natures tried and true
Shall re-arrange

Flight patterns to the south before the wind doth blow
At this point in September/ October the thought of snow
     is faux

Each breath I take of the fresh crisp fall wind
Reminds me of that special hymn/ him
To bed all sleepy heads
Be safe and warm and dream
Of days at Sleepy Hollow Lake
We shall contemplate—just you and me!

Ode To William Herbert Andrew

It is mid September, sitting in the misty rain
On the dock with my brother
Fish are bubbling but not as much as one another

Sharing news, thoughts and feelings
My brother wishes he had brought his reel
For the fish, not for our dish
But for fun

I love our time together!

Much love and appreciation for all you do!

My Heart's On Fire

The flames are reaching toward the sky
Through the chimney and onward high
The logs are attached and close
Flames embellish their bellies below

Ashes pilling high as the flames do their dance
The screen provides protection
So we can take a chance
I sit near the warmth for I am in need

I close my eyes and feel so secure
I know with this light and warmth
I shall endure
Winter's portrait of crisp and white

Please, two of us, on future cold and windy nights.

First Christmas Sleepy Hollow Lake A Special Eve For Goodness' Sake

I can now build a fire any time I wish
Unlike most of our Christmas celebrations of the past
This 98 will hold beautiful peaceful memories that will
    overrule and last
No friction, no dictation, no blasts from the aghast
This very moment in time did surpass

I usually express depression and the sadness of things
But my heart and soul has changed and we feel like bells
    that ring
Crisp, clear, precise, accurate
Sounds high and inspirational
It actually feels sensational

As a dear friend sits by my side
With pride, I glance at a relative by chance who takes time
    for laughter not sighs
No criticism to down you
No body language to frown upon you

Yes—Happy Birthday Jesus
In the name of the father the son and Virgin Mary One
God Bless, it is done by faith in the Holy Ones
A Christmas gift to cherish forever.

Happy Valentine's Day

Classical music and classic men
Do you remember when?
Courting was a message, not necessarily from just a friend
Flowers, candy, a beautiful card
Yet the message was typed— could have been words made by
That musical star

We all fell in love when we were oh so young
Every movie star was hung
Somewhere on our bedroom wall or in a scrapbook or if
     mom
Or dad permitted placement in the family hall

Marriage is indeed a special event
The love of my life has come but shortly after he is gone
May I please vent my feelings of true love so strong

First one must love oneself and not sit there sulking on the
     shelf
Take the boot by the strap and give him a good rap
I love myself therefore I love thee
How much simpler can love be?

We make things complex and thus a hex
Sign of the times but many of us now understand
It should be the love in our hearts for all our fellow man.

Trouble With Hurt Feeling

I think the trouble with hurt feelings is the trouble with you. By that I mean, how strong is your inner strength? The stronger you are and the faster you can rejuvenate yourself and get on with your life, the happier you will be. Your feelings will be complete.

Sometimes I thought of hurt feelings as an albatross around the neck. Position here, it cuts off the positive mental supply needed and it prevents mind body relationship also in a healthy way.

Hurt feelings at times have felt like a new shoe in which you start your day with pride on your feet and by the end of the day, oh how sweet to take them off.

Hurt feelings may leave for awhile and then all of a sudden with a visual or musical reminder, pop right back onto the scene of your stage in life.

Extremes in feelings are both happy and sad and these are the ones we never forget and tend not to dwell on them. With these feelings we more or less pray and they disperse.

When songs like Truckin and Devil with the Blue Dress, blue dress come on I cannot sit still. It is movement time where ever it is or whoever is there. I dance.

My favorite feeling is a hug that lasts for at least 30 seconds. It was a very special hug and feeling when Dr. Schuller from the Chrystal Cathedral in California embraced me after his signing my favorite book "Living positively one day at a time."

I have processed great sensibility. Italiano we say sympatico! The sense of touch, sensation, sensibility, emotion, sympathy— I leave you with all of these.

Fall 2004

The outgoing summer with sunsets divine
Welcome in the fall
Where corn husks are tall
The birds are still singing their favorite songs

The winds blows through the thin grass with dandelion weed
Beaver, otter, blue herons and the like
Prepare for flight or long winter nights
The pines stretch out their masterful limbs
I sit beneath wondering
Should I enjoy my last swim?

The lake waters are cold
I must be bold and float like a boat on in
Splashing and thrashing, next one to surface—a hawk
With bounty in his beak
He cannot speak
Of the exit of fall into winter

No more beautiful, brilliant colors
Just pensive brown, green and white
Blue skies upon occasion and very black at night

We must all prepare mentally and physically
For winter's walk into our lives
Filled in many ways
With an abundance of warmth and surprise!

Winter 2003

Snowflakes whirling in the wind
Touching roof tops and leaving a grin
Traced in the snow by the wind
Trees all dressed up with the appearance of white fur
Resting on the branches, berries, and greens
Indeed, such a lovely sleepy hollow lake scene

The deer and wild turkey are feasting galore
In the birdfeeders, all about magnificent birds
Blue jays, sparrows, cardinals male & female rest
On the perch and indulge in the delicacy of the best

'Tis the season to be jolly and gay
To be generous to nature and the friends in the next bay
I hear the ice skaters on our narrow cove
Greeting all with a cheery happy holidays ~ ho, ho, ho!

On cross-country skis someone delivered to me
A beautiful gift for this Christmas 2003
Excited more by the energy and effort it took
May I tell you, it was a book.

I shall read a page that I wish to share for blessings
Of the home and hearth:
"Walls for the wind
A roof for the snow
Drinks by the fireside
Laughter to cheer you
And all that your heart may desire!"

Happy holidays to all at Sleepy Hollow Lake!

Portrait Of A Lady

From the dark background
A beautiful face
Soft and pale with a touch of grace
Brown eyes searching for a place of focus
Believe me there is nothing about this fine
Lady that is bogus

A foxy lady indeed
With the very same around her neck
And touching close to her sleeve
Illuminate us with your experience, thoughts
And please do share your dreams

Shall enjoy your presence in our abode
And in our everyday scheme
You shall relax with us, infatuate us,
In you we shall esteem

Peter Jung Fine Arts was where we found you
And now may we astound you, by bringing
You, my dear lady, home.

Disappointment

I know they say
You may not always have you way
Not actually my point today
One looks at friends as people who are usually there for you
Recently I have learned that skepticism is their resounding
    voodoo
There's no need for this when all we wish for is to help

But set forth by the majority is the negative yelp
On the other hand give me a man with disappointment
I look at this as a positive deed on the part of me
Suggestion of candor, frankness, insight
To help him straighten up and fly right

I much prefer the positive attitude in life
Yet there are many who constantly through their life
Wallow in self pity, disappointment and strife

A tear now and forever whether happy or sad or
Mystifyingly glad
Cleanses the mind's eye and it is far more clear
To see

I am you and you are me
Feelings of all kinds, each moment, each day
Are meant to be!

Devotion

Devotion to a mother
Devotion to all friends
Staying in touch
And making amends
This is the way to win in the end

Peace will reign in your heart and soul
This we all need as we age and grow old

My life seems meaningless tonight
Why, I cry?
I long for tomorrow to push away the sorrow
To hold my head high
To breath a restful sigh
I will try!

These moments are unexpected
We cannot stay numb
Reach out and move along
Movement in many ways makes us strong
Do not keep your mind on one spot too long

Shift gears
Once in awhile tears
New adventures make things happen
Follow through and no more blues
Anticipate many more clues to solve the mysteries in life!

Sand / Ocean / Sky / Reflection

Deep is the footprint in the sand
Difficult to tell if it is child, woman, or man's
A work of art as the ocean ripples cascade
I see a path, a long straight braid
The tide is now out and has left us creations grand
It is up to our imaginations to decipher those
Graphics in the sand.

The truth may be told and you need not be bold
Believe in yourself as you know oceans have waves
And a shore
Be flexible as the marsh weeds that bend with the ocean
     wind
Give love and understanding, respect and responsibility
There is no room for sin.

As the ocean wave enters the shore and immediately leaves
You must enter each day with a positive rhythm of "I am me!"
Be, entertaining, truthful with joy in your heart
For you know the ocean and its shore will never part

A stable, secure, relationship is what we all need
But first within ourselves and then with god we see
For nowhere on this earth could we ever find a better
Birth than living and loving in our country
The good old united states of America

Fire Place Thoughts

Am I wasting my time?
I do not know
Am I wasting my time by the fireplace glow
As I clutch my Royal Dalton mug
Filled to the new
With sensory messages that will undoubtedly confuse

In my vessel is a warm milky taste
Lots of chocolate too and I can wait to taste
It is steaming hot sensory height
Oh, how in love I am with this night

The first sip which burns so I turn toward the flames
The logs piled so high, it is almost insane
The warmth from the hand held mug and fireplace
Put me in a trance
I close my eyes and I dance, dance, dance

Floor patterns galore shoot through my mind
In due time I shall be the choreographer divine
As I slowly open my eyes I do see
The magnificent colors of the fire thrown to me

My favorite taste and my favorite place
If only I could share it with a favorite face
The chair next to mine is empty
Being saved for an old beau
Why does this warmth open up my heart and soul

I live to share with friends and feel peace when made amends
This happens to me over and over again
There is lots of company in my mind
Years of memories, experiences which could use a good
      review
You contact me and I'll contact you.

You are never alone as I glance at that empty fireplace chair
The father, the son and the holy spirit are there as one,
      sitting there
My cocoa and fireplace seem to say
Warmth in your life is always there and there to stay

JZGT

Without the support of Jonathan, Zane, George, and
Thurley I would not today be up so early
The vim, vigor, and vitality have returned

My heart does wish to continue my work and learn
A note of gratitude for your thoughts and prayers
As I carefully return to climb the stairs
The stairs of success for you have helped my life appear
worthwhile

I can tell by your embrace, your gifts, your patience, and
your smiles

Toute suite, schnell, to all a fond embrace

Together we will battle and celebrate the wonders of life's
race.
God bless and thank you!

Gold Beads

Gold beads found at a thrift shop in town
Shall we count and feel the soft and round
Believe me they make a wonderful sound
Jingle and jangle— they shake in my hand
Do you wish to stand and dance to beat the band?

No competition with their luster
Hold them in your hand and what a beautiful cluster
Their movement is endless as they swirl about my wrist
Up and down motion with your arm will set up a
Movement with charm

Place them on the table and make the figure 8
How about an "s"
My goodness these beads are truly the best
Who would have ever guessed?

I place them on the crown of my head
A princess or queen or king instead
A circle to roll the marble up and in
Did I evoke on my friend's lips, a little grin?

With a paper clip
You have sunglasses, zip zip zip
Find some blocks or sticks
Make a lollipop, quick, quick, quick

I wish to thank the thrift shop
For such a marvelous gift
When you are down and low
Buy some beads and go— go— go!
No more low, but an awesome glow!

Growth

Growth can be simple and tremendous if we let go
Cut your stages of life
And report to yourself
It is truly balanced, forgiving, no longer blue
As I let go of the old thoughts and bring in the new.

Count your blessings and thank the dear lord each day
For your neighbor, the mayor, the politicians we pray
Long live the queen yes
But long live America the America we have seen and loved
And been with for years
The country of laughter, the country of tears.

Another thought or two may I share with you
As the last of the morning doves cuddle and coo
A glance out this window on an early morn
Dew drops on the leaves bring moisture, love not scorn

The sun burst its rays
I fall to my knees and pray
To be productive and human today.

Silence

When vexing words are said to you
Smile, and keep bravely still

Annoying tongues will have their way
Let you say what you will

Then shut your lips, speak not a word
This is the wisest plan

Silence hurts tormentors more
Than any answer can.

Silence is golden, indeed!

Too Quiet This Fall

The pitter patter of many feet
Here in the shop as I sit in my seat
At the computer that I touch each day
So quiet in the shops as the market sways

People are leery of spending a dime
Christmas in 2002 may be blue not divine
The coming of the Jesus to celebrate always sublime.

The flag says open and the door on a crack
Please enter the stairs and see the beauty within
American oil paintings, furniture and oriental kilims

We are not the only shop that is quiet and waiting
All along the block— we all are anticipating
Will there be war with Iraq or Iran
Middle East bubbling with tricks up their sleeves
Missiles, bombs, terrorism
Appears, no reprieve.

That is why our economy is slow
Our dependency on others in time should go
Self sufficient, creative, only sharing with friends
Canada, Mexico and islands in the Atlantic sea
More for you and more for me

We should share and care and find the truth
It is in giving and respect and freedom
That we find our wealth.
Antibiotics, neurotics we will cease to be
Pray for peace so we all may be!

Skaket Beach

Cape Cod's Skaket Beach
What a beautiful treat
The sun is high with a fresh east breeze by its side
The marsh weeds exude a beautiful hue
Of lime green and browns
Again the wind sweeps and the marsh weeds
Dance around
Voices whisper softly from their blankets and chairs

A view of the tip of province town
I stretch my arm to reach
It would be minutes in the air
If we could take a helicopter there

My comfort level is riding extremely high
Might I say high as we can observe the cold blue tide
Turn off your motor, erase your board, eliminate the
        negative
Who could ask for more

A magnificent day
Come and rest
Skaket beach is one of Cape Cod's very best!

The Not Forgotten Beach

Tragedy of war, indeed, hits one's mind and soul
Memories are aroused as the soldiers carouse
And loved ones at home weep and mourn

Tragedy of war makes for long time healing and making amends
Dealing with thoughts, words and actions which
Seems to have no meaning even when war ends.

An anonymous soldier may be comparable to a minute
    grain of sand
Compounded with thousands that indeed, makes our land
And next to that land is the sea
And above the sea the sky

No matter who the soldier whether living or dead they gave
    a valiant try!
Our flag represents our country which through wars fought
    and won
The battles were many and plenty as I turn my head to the sun

Each of us whether male or female may sometimes lose
    and sometimes win
Support one another should always be shared with a prayer
    and a grin
A grin that reminds us always of the sacrifices made

With this in mind we know, that under the spreading
    chestnut Tree, our children will be able to safely play.

Springtime 2004

Nature comes alive at Sleepy Hollow Lake
Springtime divine gives us all a change of mind
Our hearts swell as the blossoms grow
On our lake kayakers and canoers begin to row
Along the shore sites galore
Birds and bees and ducks and trees
Ramble on and rustle old dried leaves
The air smells fresh and the cold is gone
Time for us to travel on.
As Springtime brings us all change
Our thoughts and actions rearrange
The sap rises and the pine needles change from yellow to
        green
Our docks awaiting boats, seem to burst at their seems
Our eyes toward the heavens with thoughts serene
I cherish this small community
Of which we must always take care, for you never know when
From behind a rock or lilipad, or tree stump
You will find the Frog Prince there
Make a wish and blow the dandelion fur
"Your wish is my command for Spring to occur."
Remember that youth is a gift of nature and age is a work
        of art
I do believe for any age, Spring is about to start

Our Town Athens

Athens is beautiful and quaint
It is a small town on the Hudson River
The historic Athens Light House is at the South end
People come from all around
Tug boats, ships, motor boats, wind surfers, kayaks and canoes
     Cruise by daily for the lighthouse view.

On the west side of town the Catskill Mountains resound
In all their splendor and beauty.
Fredrick Church and Thomas Cole painted their heart and
     soul into the Catskills
Along Farm to Market Road in the summertime, you will see
Artists with their pallets, easels, brushes, and paint
Bringing to others the privilege, we have to see daily,
     magnificent.

Down from my home, I often roam, to the fields and marsh
     weed
They whisper to one another and dance in the wind like
     there is no other
I have found many a splendid scene
Look up to the sky, hawks circling for their prey
Blue heron are seen resting on the dock by the bay

Sparrows, cardinals, goldfinch galore
In the distance we observe families of wild turkey, grouse,
     rabbits and ducks

The deer leap over fences and the fox sneak around
Both issuing silence so as not to be found.

On a lazy day I go off to be inspired to the 100 year old D.
      R. Evart Library
It has books, videos, CDs, and a little shop downstairs for a
      gift or two
We have had gatherings in the meeting room— interviews,
      board meetings
and our writing class too.

Down East in Athens, a block or more is the Stewart House
Like the library, 100 years old or more
Delicious cuisine along with bed and breakfast privileges too
An outdoor bar in the summer, on the river, for a couple of
      "How do you dos"
Live music in the park, we celebrate until dark

Second Street takes us there
How did Steven Spielberg become aware of such a lovely
      place?
A perfect downhill run straight to the Hudson River, dock,
      and ship
The War of the Worlds gave many of us a superb lift.
With fond memories this has past with many more to come.
If ever you travel this way, we say "Welcome to Athens,
      New York."

That Time Of The Year

Cold and calculating she may be
Strong as an ox on land and sea
Puts on a blanket and covers herself
Melts in a moment as the sun in the sky dwells

Invisible as she enters
No bells or bows
At her time you will never hear
The crackling of the noisy crow
More of the fireplace glow

She grows in depth as time marches on
Children and adults enjoy playing with her
A constant wrap around town
She accentuates the pine and spruce
Emphasis on the Christmas goose

Red berries at this time on the trees
She welcomes the holiday season
Did you know she is winter?
And here with us, as lovely as can be!
Happy holidays to one and all!

What Do I Do

I am alone
Nowhere to go
Nothing to do
My feelings are racing
Home to you
You are not there
So what do I care
I sit and stare
God and nature are my very best friends
They shall be with me to the very end.
My loss is great but should not get me down
Possibility thinking—profound.
If you were me what would you do?
Possibility thinking for me and you
Yes, possibility thinking for me and you!

Thomas Cole

Thomas Cole and a pot of gold
Feelings overwhelmingly sublime
It has taken it's time
Two hundred years—laughter and tears

The Mountain House and lake with dead trees
The top of Katerskill Falls tells it all
I am still feeling disbelief.

Thomas and Asher B. Durand and the whole clan
Here with their fellow man
Two hundred years

Where is Maria and the children and the bears
Magnificent paintings of the Hudson River School
Many artists lead by Cole—Fredrick Church I've been told
A magnificent tool, a gift of God
I'm no fool

Uncle Sandy we thank you too for the land and house and
    all you do

To Europe, to America—call all its people and sing praise
    for Thomas Cole.

Ode To A Friend

Slow down your pressure stress and pace
Come along and join once again the human race

Participate and dream
Let your mind ramble and also scream
Pull back, relax and echo, so it seems

Have faith and pray for I am here to say
You are welcome
I am proud of you
Do not hesitate to stay

Let us see that smile
Let it linger awhile
As we wait in joyful hope

That someday soon
You will reach for the moon
And a star will be added to your tune

You are great
I cannot wait to see you again!

A Cool Adventure

Cold hands and warm hearts
Let us make a start
From underneath the surface we can see to the top
The frozen black ice is hard as a rock

Do not stand there bewildered
Enjoy a skate on top

A small fire beside
Our skates do glide
Into a figure eight
My oh my does it feel great

To have support beneath us
Makes it capable for one to be on top
A good foundation is the one I choose a lot.

A cup of cocoa and friends with which to share
The cold yet warmth beyond compare

The clouds do ramble before us
A forecast of heavy snow
No more skating for awhile
But that is the way northeastern winters go!

25th Coxsackie River Festival

"Owl" be seeing you at the Riverside Festival
We will be celebrating our 25th year
There will be music to bring great cheer to our ears

The Native American term for Coxsackie is "hoot of an
     owl"
We are not trying to play foul (fowl) or even growl
Just trying to enhance you to come hoot and howl

You will be able to Dutch Apple cruise down the river
We may even target a bow and a quiver

Games for the children
Good food, crafts and such
You all will enjoy the Coxsackie River Festival's 25th
Oh so very much

T-shirts with an owl motif for sale
Fireworks in the evening
We might just even offer this year pale ale

So bring family and friends and even a pen
To autograph the commencement and end of a fabulous
Coxsackie river festival 25th year

Oh my dear! It was wonderful— here, hear!

Pourquoi

Why are some people kind and interested
Why are some people not

Why are some people cold and calculating
Why are some people hot

Why are some people selfish and critical
Why do some people give and care

Why do we have pollution to contend with
Why not pure fresh air

Why do people not answer your questions
They negate and glance with a stare

Why are there more frowns than smiles
Why to get anywhere do we have to walk a mile

Why is commitment such a frightening thing
Why not live, love, and learn with a heart that sings
Why not enjoy a pleasing spring!

Nature Speaks

Just step outside and you shall feel how warm within
Breathe fresh air— observe the moon and clouds above

There are messages to be seen and felt
The wind and trees also breathe a message to thee
Fortunate we are, to use our mind to unwind
The peaceful white snow and with the moon's glow
I truly begin to know
If you wish the answers to a peaceful life
No remorse, no strife

God has a plan for you and your wife

Go outside on a moonlit night
Observe
At nature, stare
The answer for your mind and soul will be there!

Generations To Come

Our lives depend on a positive trend
In Greene and Columbia counties the beauty of nature
    never ends
Forest glades, birds singing sweetly, lofty mountains grandeur

Hear the waters of the river and feel the gentle breeze
Olana in sight, each letter of her name
Brings to all nature's historic fame

Oh—the beauty of ponds and lakes
Land of which God makes no more and no mistakes
Abundant fields of grain due to
Non Acidic rain

We want generations, not generators to live and live and
    live again
No smoke stacks in the sky
Only trees and human minds should run high
Generating stacks, do they not deprive us all

Of a healthy summer, winter, spring and fall?

DEPRIVATION

    DEGRADTION

        CONTEMPLATION/SITUATION

      STOP

The New Year Message

We had hoped to see the stars last night
Instead there were clouds that covered the light

Jupiter near Orion was suppose to be
The most spectacular sight but we were unable to see

Disappointment so often comes our way
Shall I embrace it or rather say

I shall look forward to the next time
Right now I shall begin
By embracing an attitude that is positive within

Life goes by so swiftly, an amazing race
Many of us have approached mid life's pace

Each New Year rings
With magnificent strings
Just pull one you shall be surprised
Just pull another and you may rise

With the highest of hopes, and faith and deeds
In loving ways we shall always succeed.

To peace and love this 2002!

Departure

Jonathan has become part of my heart and soul
In leaving our work together I must be bold
Find a space to help their place
It may never be the same yet that is called change

I walk right now among the crowd
In hopes of standing out
I interview and find a crew with which I find no doubt

It takes time to search for that special perch
That one will sit upon
With energy effort day after day
You, indeed, will find your way

The door has opened for us as we enter in
Closed behind us but memories will stay akin
Enjoy each day and learn your way through life's
Challenging feats
I loved every minute at 438 ½ Warren Street
A treat to beat your feet

But now I must go and try not to show the tears
That drop from my eyes.
They are filled with the salt of experience
And in life I shall continue to try.

Our quiet environment shall dissipate
Onward to action with no abate
God bless!

The Approach Of The Fall Season

Small round circles appear on the lake
By fishes kissing lips— make no mistake
The sun is brilliant on the tree tops
A show of falls beginning, yet it is the end of day

Quiet and calm is the water
Whispers of crickets about to adjourn
Motors are up on the party boats
Canoes resting on top of the dock
Wish I could sit on the edge forever
And not always live by the clock

A small two-seater flies low in the sky
Its engine is humming as it glides by with such pride
Would it not be lovely if it landed to give us a ride

A magnificent October day
For this we always pray
The chill of the air is encouraging a stare
As my eyes gaze at the water and absorb the reflection
Six geese in v formation parade above

The blue jays call for their family for which they love
Darkness is here so gather for warmth that is near
God bless nature who holds our hand
And gives to us always that which is grand!

A Gentle Northeast Rain

Pitter patter pitter patter
Watch the rain do its best to splatter
A tap tat tap
A rhythm as such
We need and should enjoy the sound
Attempt to feel its touch

The rain drops cleanse
The birds do bath
The air is clean and a new soil ridge is made
The water flows from head to toe
The ground absorbs from every pore

This relished staple of need
It supports the seed, even the tangled weed, take heed
Rain is a precious gift from above
Without this gift— no bath, no christening, no love

For the plan is such
That we should yearn to touch
The pitter patter pitter patter splash
The moisture that is indeed our crutch

The splatter has a calming effect
Having trouble keeping my eyes open and my neck erect
It is time now for that Sleepy Hollow snooze
I am about to indulge in a delightful rain swept sleep cruise.

To Tell The Truth

I feel a little bit like gloom, in a tomb, looking forward to
    the full moon
There is an absence I can not explain, in vain, and I hope I
    do not go insane
I have apologized which I think was wise but somehow he
    may think there is disguise

Not true as I explain to you all I have done to heel the wound
It has been open for years, many a tear, incredible fear, will
    you lend your ear
The new century has bought all together, the problem is
    solved
No more whining and I shall not crawl

Trust is the key to everything, in the Lord and each other
Let no man put asunder
I usher in new thoughts that are positive not bereaved
With such thoughts I AM relieved

Will you come along with me and have some tea?

Recovery

I am on the mend
I will tell you when-a week ago
Pain and panic— one becomes manic
It will not go away
Moan and pray— moan and pray

Speed to the side of cure
Will I endure, will I endure?
Arrival is no guarantee
Fourteen hours on emergency room time
Short staffed, yes short handed
Will I lose my mind?

A brother's comfort is mighty fine
At the time, I would say divine!

Diagnosis, relief at last
Off for operation on the slab
Confidence in my doctor, I have
The size of a robin's egg, he did say
As I recuperate from surgery the previous day

The "gall" in my life is gone
The bladder, does it matter?
Time to sing a different song.

Acute awareness of foods and exercise
Might along with the help of God
Bring to me a life surprise— more time

To your Health!
It is Wealth in this world of ours!

The Holiday Season

Tis the holiday season filled with joy
For every man, women, girl and boy
Gifts of love are given in time
Oh how she loved her book of rhyme

Love fills the air and climbs the stairs
Where the children sleep and dream of little Bo Peep
There are sounds on the roof top
I know he is there
Instead of the chimney that is filled with warmth
He may climb the stairs

The spirit within us all
Should hear the sound and call
Over mountain top and hill
There is peace and goodwill

The spirit of the season
Should extend throughout the year
Can be spread to rich and poor
And to those who endure the hardships of life

It is in giving that we receive
Thus very little time should be devoted to the process of
        grieve Conceive, relieve

The feeling of peace of mind is the richest of its kind
God Bless ye merry gentlemen
And a Happy New Year!

Ode To Renew 2000

God is with us no matter where we go
Raking the leaves or plowing snow
The seed that we plant lay dormant for awhile
As we with our thought, our actions, our smiles

Transformation of the seasons tap lightly on the seed's
    door
Do you wish to grow, so as to do more?
Yes, for yourself be proud and bloom and show
Bring happiness to others as the sun doth glow

Even when it is cold or raw with rain
WE gather your bouquet, whether it be thoughts or flowers
To many we shall say

Yes, it is dreary sometimes, but you have brought me some
    light
Some new beauty, some fragrance, some new peace,
    although slight
Merely a drop of rain will help the seed to grow
With hours of showers imagine it so . . . .

Big dreams, big thoughts, big desires
Help to eradicate the negative fires
Our positive attitude
      Planted by God
           Hang on to it
                Nurture it
                     Give HIM Laud!

Yes, praise to the heavens and the earth
Spring forth with your, your light, your birth!

Amen.

Love

Am I dead or alive?
See my circle of life!
Stem's end to the center
Strength and love keep me together

Turned brown leaves
I am proud to display
Many years of effort you see today

A life of struggle
In addition much love
I am still seeking attention

Love is the stem of all life
It feeds to many and at some point retracts
Yet it's there always for those who reach out

Thank you for your attention and admiration
Even at this stage of life
The chestnut tree branch

Whatever I Am Feeling

Whatever I am feeling
I am feeling it with pride
I sit by the candle light
And breathe a wishful sigh
Could I really be feeling so special inside?

My heart and soul
For many years have been cold
It is the quality of humor that helps me unfold
I fell in love once— until death do we part
I thought we had a good start

A life together in fair and stormy weather
Instead he decided we were not birds of a feather
Oh— come on and get yourself together
It is just impossible to do or undo
I must say I am still very fond of you

It takes time to heal
Before you can sincerely rock and reel
A special friend to share your cares and woes
Is it possible to say "here we go!?"

I will listen, laugh and learn
As your heart does truly yearn
You too, again, cannot care or love
Until you have spoken and prayed with our spirit high above

He is the one love always there to guide you
Stand beside you
Through thick and thin
He will help you face the world with your handsome grin

When do you start? You start now!
Glance toward the sky and you're bound to see clouds
Yet among them is the sun
A measure of warmth and light
You shall never be alone— morning noon or night

A roll in the hay may be fun in a way
But momentary only, I say
Become good friends first and in the end
With your heart and soul you shall whisper a peaceful amen
Whatever I am feeling— may I feel it again!

Up And Down The Street

Up and down the street we see the pitter patter of many
    feet
Heads stand tall and some hung low
How on earth do the latter know where to go? Black, Asian,
    White take flight from day to night
Up and down the street
Are they cruising or what?

One with the newspaper and an umbrella
One with a huge bag of stuff
Shoulders hunched
Pocketbooks slung
Thank goodness there is no one seen with a gun

Cars too go by on the fly
The big bopper with car windows down
Just listen to those awesome sounds

Deliveries made by a volunteer not paid
Child in arm carried so no harm, strong arms
Back and forth, forth and back
There is no one with a gunny sack

Laboring eyes on the window pane do fall
Would they like to enter, just wave or call
Heavy set with a tilted head
One, two, three, four in a family row
Time for off to bed we go.

Looking forward, looking back
Up and down the street
The pitter patter of many feet.

Forty Steps

The leaves have fallen on the ground
The ocean is quiet— not even a sound
The wind's at my back with a gentle push
The sea gulls play a gleeful game
in the marsh weeds and the bush.
The sounds of the leaves
They rustle by with swift pace
My soul rises to the surface,
mid life's race.
The need for 40 more steps to untie past disgrace.
The misty horizon makes it clear
That adventure, the unknown will
        always appear.
The bay of tranquility rests before me,
        not an ocean of storm
There are people so dear and
        so near and so warm.
Fresh is the air that I breath
Clear is my mind as I think
Let us all be so grateful for God's
        plan for our lives
I am a human being with spirit
I am God's given man.
We who try to slide by showing
        never a cry

Do not succeed but become
a weed—tangled,
　　torn, rooted and
　　　　such—
I am not that way anymore.
I've changed—thanks Dear Lord
　　so much.

I Wonder

One mound of snow left on the lawn
One mound of feelings gone— forlorn
The wind is brisk
I feel its threat
An afternoon I shall never forget

It is hard to go back into the past
Today it presented itself
Will those feelings last
The sound of his voice made me say
You sound so different in every way

It has been many years since his embrace
I must redefine my plan
No longer with him but on my own
I appreciate his being but no longer my song

I would love to visit and catch up on many years gone by
Come to my house, relax, and feel free
To say or do anything with me and family

God bless— the feeling must rest.
I wonder?

A Cold Spring

A cold spring is on this earth
No one, not a thing is warm to give birth
I challenge my mind to bring forth the new
But always go back to when I was blue

I never fail to project the past
I wonder how long this will last
I donate to the Native Americans and it makes me feel good
I work on my house which is made purely of wood

I need inspiration from something as small as a fallen rose
Then, indeed, I can compose
The most beautiful thoughts you could ever dream
As beautiful and tasty as peaches and cream

I can do it right sometimes and at others do it wrong
It's human nature and creativity to compose a song
A song that will last forever more
Like the song I wrote for Tony Bennet and left it on his
      door.

No response
You never give up
But try on your positive attitude and you can not go wrong
Turn your scars into stars
And life will always be
Up and available for you and for me.

Our River

The river's reflection on my face
Recall the meaning of mid life's race
A wonderful setting to contemplate

A handsome crane glides by and onto the shore
On river's edge there are many more
The tugs push barges upstream and down
The geese gather their wits about them
As the barge goes around

The wind is brisk so the waves slap the shore
Motor boats go by with a piercing roar
Underneath the schimmering I can see
Schools of fish, rock, and weed

Marsh weeds grow
The river flows
Waves abound
Hear the river's sound

For many miles the river flows
Its smell as delightful as fresh water from a well
Bridges connect so we may go
From shore to shore
And town to town
The river's life can be found

From North to South
And East to West
The Dear Lord's creation is at its best!

Colors

Colors of beige, sage, and brown
As our favorite Spring rolls around
Marsh weeds, bushes, and our beloved green grass
All are ready to green in for cash

Their cash is showing off and dancing in the wind
Oh how I yearn for Spring to begin
They change their whole attire from a small seed in the
    ground
To a red rose of fire

Off to the Lake to escape
Yes, the roses are in bloom
Singing a very fragrant tune
Come join in the colors and blooms of Spring
Then you will not have missed a thing.

Patience Is A Virtue

Spit bullets I wish I could
Aim it at that nasty lady who said I should
I could be next in line and three have past
Hike out in rough waters I would love to do in my craft

Let the wind fill the sail
Let us bail, bail, bail
As the rain comes down as hard and fast as it can
Man overboard, hit the deck, land ho and away we go

I grasp the brass rail so hard I bent my ring
I feel like shouting not anything to sing
Deep breaths and pull on the sail
The wind is dying and so am I

I never got my turn so I must continually learn
To let Go and let God
Then the patience will come and stay with you until the day
        is done
And forever more.

Ode To Winter Fair:
A Trip To White Rice On
A Snowy Winter Night

Winter has arrived cold and raw
Still hear those black birds caw
White rice doors open
Many people come flocking in
A look see hear
And a look-see there
Floating serious nary a care

Holidays are upon us
One must shop until one drops
Beauty in white rice feels good and is pure
Handmade by Balinese sanded round and square
There is in existence everything there

Curves and light
There is Santa in sight with reindeer and all their might
Pulling the sleigh that just may swing their direction your way
Caroling, tree trimming and angels in the snow
White rice on this winter night
To Hudson we must go!

Merry Christmas!!!!!!!!!!!!!!!!!!!!!!!!!!!

Our Man

Inauguration 2009
Barack Obama divine
TV NBC, CBS
Radio Stations all the
best Reporting on the
coming event Money,
indeed, well spent

Obama is a special man
Inspirational— Sensational
Certainly in great demand
I have this feeling in my heart
Obama will set us apart

Government is the problem
Yes, apart shall bring us change
And hope for all concerned
Change in our country
Change what is wrong with America
By what is right with America

Change our minds, hearts and souls
It starts with one being
Moves on to millions more

God Bless America
God Bless our man
Everyone has to be involved
Are we ready— yes we are
To see what the country can be
Obama you're our man— move as swiftly as you can!

Someone

Someone bakes the pies
Someone tells the lies
Someone gives all he can
Someone does not understand

Someone cares
Someone dares
Someone is complete
Someone stands on their own two feet

Someone flies
Someone dies
Someone is responsible
Someone is not

Someone dates
Someone smokes
Someone rings the bell
Come in dear friend and rest
Someone did their best!

Victor

I am a victor, not a victim
I have the favor of God
Throw your shoulders back
Put a smile on your face
And sing the praises of the Lord
I am blessed
I am creative
I have something from within.
The seed that God planted
Is with me to the end
Who told you you do not have what it takes to succeed?
Who told you something was wrong with you?
Those are lies from the enemy
You need to reject
God's gifts and his callings are irrevocable
God is never going to take them back
He can do the same for you
You have incredible potential within
Tap it— snap it— strap it to your being
And expect good only to share
A change of heart and a change of scene
In the end will reign supreme!

Friendship

The gusts of wind keep flushing through
My memories are of me and you
The Cape is delightful at every season
I always attend for a special reason
My friends like family are here
Hospitality, friendship and love are always near

Seymour Pond is across the way
A skinny dip in store on this delightful day
The antique shops with awesome paintings, Royal Dalton
     and more
Would it not be nice to open up my own store.

The birds are fed with suite and seed
In and out of the feeder they constantly take heed
The petunia plant is dancing with the wind
It certainly does evoke a grin

I will be sad to leave
And happy to know
Next year at this time where will I go, you know.

Attitude

He entered the door with a smile on his face
I made a request and it was simply erased
It has to be his way for he is in charge
Go on with your life and float like a barge

The care and feelings for others did not show
Go go go get out of here
Leave me with my wife and life

The social network is right at hand
Golf buddies, tennis buddies, to beat the band
I had a good time and believe me you friends are divine
You may not know or show them kind
Maybe in time.

Rigid, frigid at the door
Negative attitude at the scene no more
There is always hope and good you will see
If you remain friends with me.

Cloudy

I feel a bit separated
It is hard to explain
Like a cloudy and sunny day being
Exactly the same
'Tis the end of summer
Beginning of fall
The fish are jumping for bugs
And the tree frogs call

There is emptiness and depression setting in
I force myself to smile, but only a grin
Deep within a stir of sorts
Big black spider on the dock caught my eye
Can you imagine if I were a meager fly
Sunning myself, then gulp

The lake is still beautiful
The trees have not changed
A turtle before me and he dives below
A breeze at my back
Cool enough to say
Keep your head about you
Stay the course
One meager unpleasant feeling
Will not ruin your life
Time passages is our real deal, our choice

Day by day
Out with the kinks
Soon for all to be in the pink.

Your Guess

It has to be easy
It cannot be hard
It is malleable
It is sensitive
It is easily carved

It can be upset in a moment's time
It is forever sublime
It has some age
At which stage I am not sure
It sends out feelings
It can be heard

I am speaking of my heart and soul
Of which you may be a part, any day of the year!

Feelings From My Heart and Soul

Feelings from my heart and soul cover the world
Feelings from my heart and soul extend to the poor and
     lonely Feelings
from my heart and soul go on forever
Feelings from my heart and soul reach out to land and sea
     Feelings
from my heart and soul never pretend to be
We all must realize
We are unique and special people
Who have been put on this earth to love and serve the Lord
     and one another
The seeds are planted by God
From my heart and soul I am grateful to be able to share all
     that is dear to me.

After An Evening Delight

After an evenings delight
It is right
Three martinis for you and for me to show
I feel as high as the sky can go
Once you are up it is hard to get down
Quiet please, nary a sound
A lobster and a salad will cool my jets
How about tomorrow , a repeat of the best !

Dear Dan

Dear Dan and I have been friends since God knows when
We go back in time
We have gone through the ridiculous and the sublime
Our destiny we never know
Yet our journey onward must go go go
Life gets complicated yet is stimulated by friends
Positive and negative the road may never end
Yet we are aboard and we adore our truest friend THE LORD
Stay peaceful and well I shall ring the bell in our honor.

My Home

A little cottage by the lake
A home for one for goodness sake
Its walls high and wide and wooden too
Its patio windows slide if you want to come thru

Wreaths and flowers and delightful plants
Horse memorabilia to accent the celebration of Derby Day
Baskets and pumpkins for Halloween I say
A Royal Dalton collection that has come my way

An old icebox and brown bottles and a portrait of Dad that
      is grand
End of Day Vase, a pair of Staffordshire Dogs, Stuben glass
      vase
And many more
Delightful things that may momentarily make your heart
      sing

But truly it is God and Man our plan for life
The giving and caring and absence of strife
Celebrate your home as I do now
But for the good Lord and Friends we take bow

Gratitude and Attitude are here to stay
Make them positive in every way
Visit my home and I will let you roam to your hearts content
For together we have been heaven sent.

Once Upon A Time

Once upon a time
It was on my mind
Prince Charming – devine
I never thought he would be that kind
    Dinners out
    Race tract gigs
    Summers on the Cape
What a great escape all the time
    Go carts
    Corvette
    MGTD 1955
Swimming and golf and racquet ball you and me
Where are we going I say
You found another lady on this day
Come to Florida and we will talk, squawk, balk
It is over ---- goodbye------ do not cry !

The Edge

A BRISK COLD November and the wind is blowing strong
A brisk cold November and where did I go wrong
Work is important and I must do what I am told
Work is very important and I can not be bold

The seagulls line up patiently here at the rivers edge
They wait for the wind to go
The sun is setting and the clouds move in
Time for us to go for a spin

I need your help DEAR LORD
No more dissention among the ranks
With you Dear Lord I will be very frank
I love Rudy my supervisor and the White Rice Store
Disobedience no more !

I am sorry and shall improve and plan to now get in the
        groove
I hope its not too late for we have had many a debate
Shall get it straight or else I tumble thus no time at all for
        a rumble
I am alive and straight and will be great,   you will see !

The Waterfalls

The water falls upon the leaves
Just to please and just to tease
The birds in their nests can"t seem to get rest
As the water falls from the leaves onto their nest

There is a time for everything and everything has its place
No race in time for all is sublime
My minds at ease
No one around to tease
The water falls its time to rest
Yes indeed you did your very best.   God Bless!

Water from the Sink

Just plain water out of the sink
Is it purple or is it pink?
No it is clear and fresh like the ringing of a bell
The water is simply cool , calm, collected and swell

We can wash the baby in it for she will love the feel
Would it not be cute to put her in a water wheel
Little buckets full to the new go round and round
Until you feel like you,

"I would love to splash" , the baby said
Splashes outward and inward and up above my head
Bubbles were added to the water and you can see
How in love the baby was with me.
A towel for drying and a little bit of crying
Yet how much baby enjoyed her first bath.

To My Family and Friends

I wish to extend to my family and friends
My gratitude and gratefulness to the end
Your fellowship, generosity, kindness and love
Will travel with me now and on to the above

I thank you for my Birthday Celebration and all you've done
For me in life
You have eased the pain and loosened the strife
And made me want to celebrate life

To grow old is to pass from passion to compassion
I leave this thought with you
Am ever so grateful for all of you my friends
Many thanks for helping me enjoy a wonderful life

Let's celebrate!!!
God Bless you!!!

Love,

Andy

You

It is almost one and we are having fun by the riverside
The sun is coming out so time to shout and play
The leaves are falling on the ground
Quiet is the sound and wow look at that wagon with hay

Pumpkins sitting on their perch
Watch the fisherman fish with a sudden lurch
He caught one and is elated indeed
Dinner for the family and leftovers maybe for me

Sailboats and motorboats and huge vessels with oil
Travel down to the city so nothing gets spoiled
I wish we could swim in the Hudson I say with a grin
PCBs and other chemicals lie within
Being washed out by it truly was a dreadful sin

Above the river is the city of Hudson itself
Many lovely shops and restaurants that make you melt
I bought a hat and scarf and some beautiful coasters
Now it is time to be a boaster

Martini time and I must go
Come join me for a sip and I will tell you for the show.